Catch Me & Kiss Me
& Say It Again

Catch Me & Kiss Me & Say It Again

RHYMES BY CLYDE WATSON

PICTURES BY WENDY WATSON

PHILOMEL BOOKS
New York

Text copyright © 1978 by Clyde Watson
Illustrations copyright © 1978 by Wendy Watson
Published in the United States by Philomel Books,
a division of The Putnam Publishing Group,
51 Madison Avenue, New York, NY 10010.
Originally published in the U.S.A. by
William Collins Publishers, Inc., 1978.
All rights reserved.
Printed in the United States of America.

Library of Congress Cataloging in Publication Data
Watson, Clyde. Catch me & kiss me & say it again.
SUMMARY: Thirty-two rhymes for the very young
including counting rhymes, lullabies, and games.
1. Nursery rhymes [1. Nursery rhymes.
2. American poetry]   I. Wendy Watson.   II. Title
PZ8.3.W28Cat   398.8   78-17644
ISBN 0-399-20948-4   ISBN 0-399-20954-9 (pbk.)

For
Mary Cameron
and
Jamie McLeod

1 2   3 4   5 6 7
All good children go to heaven
7 6   5 4   3   2 1
Naughty children have more fun

The sun came up this morning
And chased the stars away
Then kissed my poppet on the nose
With a How-do-you-do-today?

Put a piggy in a poke
Zig zag zed
Up he comes & in a twinkle
Out pops his head

A hat to warm your topknot
And boots to warm your toes
A zipper, a button
A buckle, a snap
All set & ready to go

Catch me & Kiss me & Say it again
Set sail in a cockleshell boat
If no one fell out
Then who stayed in?
Catch me & Kiss me & Say it again

Cobwebs, Cobwebs
Upstairs & down
Brush them away & let's have a look
At the prettiest pearls in town

Sing a song of soapsuds
Filling up the sink
Five & five a-washing
Quick as a wink
When the water's dirty
Send it down the drain
Curlie-wurlie, there it goes
& shan't be seen again

Butterprint knocks on the milkshop door
What will he have today?
A rosebud, a dumpling
A nipperkin of milk
Then Butterprint's on his way

Clip-clop, clippity-clop
Ride a cock-horse to the fair
All the people along the way
Look up to see who's there

Giddy-up Dobbin, giddy-up hey
Let's go a little bit faster!
Trit-trot, trit-trot
The little horse minds his master

But all of a sudden, a-gallop a-gallop
Something has made him take fright
Up & down & all over the place
Hold on with all your might!

Whoa there, whoa Dobbin
Here's the fair at last
Corey shall have a cranberry tart
And you shall have sweet green grass

Do the baby cake-walk
A one-step, a two-step
A wobble & a bobble in the knee,
With a toe heel toe
And a giddy-go-round you go
Won't you do the baby cake-walk
For me?

Handy-dandy, maple candy
Which hand do you choose?
Hand with something in, you win
But empty hand you lose

Handy-dandy, maple candy
Which hand do you pick?
Dilly-dally, shilly-shally
Choose one & be quick

Here comes a mouse
Mousie, mousie, mouse

With tiny light feet
And a soft pink nose
Tickledy tickle
Wherever he goes

He runs up your arm
And under your chin
Don't open your mouth
Or the mouse will run in

Mousie, mousie, mouse!

One, one
Cinnamon bun

Two, two
Chicken stew

Three, three
Cakes & tea

Four, four
I want more

Five, five
Honey in a hive

Six, six
Pretzel sticks

Seven, seven
Straight from heaven

Eight, eight
Clean your plate

Nine, nine
Look at mine

Ten, ten
Start over again!

Cockyolly Bumkin merry go bet
Fell in the duckpond & got all wet
A nickel for a nappy & a penny for a pin
To dress my little Cockyolly Bumkin in

This little pig found a hole in the fence
This little pig jumped through
This little pig headed straight for the garden
This little pig did too
This little pig said, Wee, wee, wee—Look what I see!

This little pig said, Mmm—juicy berries
This little pig said, Nice sweet lettuce
This little pig said, Here comes the farmer!
This little pig said, Better run or he'll get us!
This little pig said, Wee, wee, wee—can't catch me!

Phoebe in a rosebush
Phoebe in a tree
There's many a Phoebe in the world
But you're the one for me

Down derry down, my Pippin my Clown
Upset the apple-cart going to town
But we'll pick up the apples & dust off your hat
And sing, All fine & dandy-o! just like that

Fee, Fie, Fo, Fum
A gingerbread baby
Come, dearie, come
First I'll eat the fingers
And then I'll eat the toes
Yes sirree sirrah, sir
And the cherry for a nose

Thumbkin Bumpkin, jolly & stout
Peter-into-Mischief roundabout
Long-and-lanky
Hanky-panky
Pinky Pinky Pirlie Winky
Rum tum tiddly dinky

Snip snap moonslivers
One by one:
Thumbkin...
Peter...
Long-and-lanky...
Hanky-panky...
All done

Off we go on a piggyback ride
Far & fancy-free
Around the world on an empty purse
And back in time for tea

Peep-eye
Where am I?
Hiding from my wily pie

Peek-a-boo
Barley broo
You can't see me
But I see you

BOO!

Clapcake, Clapcake
Butter & Milk
Honey & Ginger
Whipped to Silk
Oatmeal, Cornmeal
A penny-pinch of Flour
Clap us out a Clapcake
And bake it for an hour

One for me & one for you
If there's one left over then what'll we do?
Take up a knife & cut it in two
So there's one for me & one for you

Here is the Nose that smelled something sweet
And led the search for a bite to eat

Here are the Feet that followed the Nose
Around the kitchen on ten Tiptoes

Here are the Eyes that looked high & low
Till they spotted six pans sitting all in a row

Here are the Arms that reached up high
To bring down a fresh-baked blueberry pie

Here is the Mouth that opened up wide
Here are the Hands that put pie inside

Here is the Tongue that licked the tin
And lapped up the juice running down the Chin

Here is the Stomach that growled for more
Here are the Legs that ran for the door

Here are the Ears that heard a whack
Here is the Bottom that felt a smack!

Tambourine, tambourine
Elves a-dancing on the green
Hand in hand & toe to toe
Round the fairy ring we go

Tambourine, tambourine
Circle round the king & queen
Down we fall & here we lie
And watch the world go spinning by

Here comes a tidbit
Open the trap-door
Gobble it, gobble it, all gone
And clap your hands for more

Once upon a time there was an old goat
He found a silver dollar in the lining of his coat
He went to the store to see what he could find
And he hemmed & he hawed till he made up his mind

At last he bought a painted cup
And a nipper of nantz to fill it up
But as he started down the stair
He tripped & went flying through the air

Cracked his elbow
Bumped his head
Hobbled home &
Went to bed

Achy bones
Broken cup
Silver dollar
All used up

No more money
Left to spend
No more story left
The end

Jagged light, blue & bright
Flashes in the air
Rumble bumble, crash boom
What's going on up there?

The Man in the Moon is having a party
Fireworks burst & fly
As wild drums & dancing feet
Echo through the sky

Rub-a-dub-dub
Fishy in a tub
Swimming for the deep blue sea
Dig for the oyster
Dive for the clam
And then come back to me

Hup! two three four
Marching out the castle door
Left right, left right
In the middle of the night
Hup! two three four
On our way to Baltimore
Left right, left right
By firefly & candle light

Hushabye my darling
Don't you make a peep
Little creatures everywhere
Are settling down to sleep

Fishes in the millpond
Goslings in the barn
Kitten by the fireside
Baby in my arms

Listen to the raindrops
Singing you to sleep
Hushabye my darling
Don't you make a peep

All tucked in & roasty toasty
Blow me a kiss good-night
Close your eyes till morning comes
Happy dreams & sleep tight

WENDY and CLYDE WATSON are sisters, two of eight multitalented children of a well-known poet and a distinguished illustrator and book designer. Their early years were spent on a farm in Vermont, where they developed an appreciation for country living, and shared with their brothers and sisters the pleasures of growing up in a lively, loving and creative family.

CLYDE WATSON is an artist, a mathematician and a professional musician, in addition to being the author of several outstanding books for children, including the beloved *Father Fox's Pennyrhymes* (illustrated by her equally famous sister, Wendy) which was an ALA Notable book and a runner-up for the National Book Award.

WENDY WATSON has illustrated more than forty books for children, some of which she also wrote herself, such as the delightful picture book *Has Winter Come?* The pictures she has made for *Catch Me & Kiss Me & Say It Again* are as warm and deliciously satisfying as home-baked bread. Executed in watercolor and grease pencil, they tell stories of their own of American family life, adding a new dimension to the joyful rhymes.